Kavi

Aadithi Arasu

Kavi

Aadithi Arasu

pblishing.com
write • share • connect • publish

KAVI by Aadithi Arasu

Published by www.pblishing.com

pblishing.com
write • share • connect • publish

Marketed by

Maple Press Private Limited
sales office A 63, Sector 58, Noida 201 301, U.P., India
phone +91 120 455 3581, 455 3583
email info@maplepress.co.in
website www.maplepress.co.in, www.maplelibrary.com

ISBN: 978-81-93324-85-1

Cover Design by **Flying Trees Private Limited**
Cover photo credit **Shutterstock.com**

Printed in India

10 9 8 7 6 5 4 3 2 1

contents

Author's note

According to me, poetry is a connection between my inner self and the outer world. Every one of my poems has a story of its own, but not a story of me.

I began writing poems at the age of twelve, but I never even dreamt of them being published, so I'd like to thank everyone who has been a part of this book. I hope you enjoy it!

- Aadithi

Prologue

This book contains thirty six poems of the most varied and random topics. They may seem sad but are definitely a joy to read.

Most of the time, happiness and sorrow go hand in hand with sorrow empowering the happiness, and this book is no exception…

Poems

SCARS

The scars you see,
The ones you mocked,
The ones you humored,
The ones you never took seriously,
They have seen the real me.
The real me, that crumbles.
The me, that's been through pain,
Pain that shatters you,
Shatters you like glass,
Glass that cannot be mended.
This hand has experienced the touch
That no girl wants voluntarily,
The touch that terrorizes you
And yet, you mocked them.
You humored them.
You never took them seriously.

Drifting

The leaves crumble beneath
The wind freezes my open chest
Metal leaves scars on my leg
Nails dig into my neck
Teeth bite into my cheek
Roughness pulling at my hair
My insides profusely bleed
And yet, I smile
Tears dampen my face because of pain
And yet, I smile
Thinking about the spring flowers
How they were planted
How they bloomed
How they smiled
A small girl ran among them
Making the petals dance as they fly free
Creating an aromatic surrounding
And suddenly, snapping back to reality
A content smile splitting my face
And soon, I feel nothing.

High Hopes

The world keeps spinning
And when it all come to an end
I'll walk with me head help high
When I tell the world
All their high hopes have been fulfilled
With a loud and clear voice filled
Filled with confidence and happiness
But no one bothers to ask
If mine have been fulfilled too
So I quietly whisper to myself
With a small and sad smile
That I will fulfill them
And run the world the same way
Yelling that I am happy
Because the only hope I have
Is that I'll be happy someday
And smile without any reason

Once Again

Try to protect the love
The love you have for yourself
The admiration you have for your laugh
The talent you have with a pen
The sound you have with music
And the hatred you have for hatred
Because not once again will you get
A person you loves you so much
You love yourself
The admiration you have for your laugh
That you never cry again
The talent you have with a pen
That you never sit idle again
The sound you have with music
That you'll always sing and elate your surrounding
And the hatred you have for hatred
That you love the smallest things about everything you do.

Morning Mourning

I wake up every morning,
Feeling the empty space beside me
Resembling the emptiness inside my heart.
I wake up every morning
Imagining your fur against my skin
Showing the warmth you always radiated
I wake up every morning
Reminiscing your paw
On my rough, hurt, wounded hand.
I wake up every morning
Looking at the shiny glass beholding your face
But the face was on paper.
I wake up every morning
Missing your sloppiness on my face
Ears drooping by the sides of my neck.
And every day, I'm getting used to this morning mourning.

Let Go

As blood trickled down her leg
She stood up
From the firm grip holding her down
She wriggled her hand free
From the metal like grip on her wrist
She shook her head
Her brown locks flying wildly
To release the stones knotting them together
She stretched her limbs
Ignoring the various cracking sounds her bones make
Getting ready for the battle
She laid punch by punch
Tears now taking place of the blood
Remembering every gaping wound
Reliving every painful moment
She let go as cool metal penetrates through
Through layers of flesh that underwent struggle.

CHANGING

As the snow settles down on branches
She walks in multiple layers
Kicking the snow out of her way
Her tears freezing as they roll down
Her hands blue with the atmosphere
Her eyes red with tears.
As she sees the roads clear of snow
Being replaced by new flowers
A new found happiness grows inside
A new curve forming on her face
Things she never knew existed.
As rain drops fall on her clothes
She spreads her arms like wings
Forming them the way she knew
Making her look different
She moved beautifully as if escaping
She knew her sadness would resurface soon.

DAD

Are you back home dad?
I can hear your laugh as a light shows on your face
A reflection rather
A reflection of a shiny surface with my face
A photo you found on the bed
The bed you were going to sleep in.
Silently I watch you as a tear falls down my cheek
Thinking about how happy you actually are
And doubting my worth in the future
And if I'd be able to keep you the same.
The falls on my chain
And causes a cold impression on my collar bone
And walk backwards as your laugh fades
Fades into the room's closure
And lay down on my bed
Thinking about you over and over again.

The Shock of The fall

Wind gushes into my ears
And my vision is black as I drop
Drop above as if from God's hands
The shock of the fall seems to hit me now
As if someone dropped a stone in my path
And immediately, I go rigid
Rigid as the same stone that I thought hit me
Rigid as a my willpower to live
But does that happen?
I am unaware, how did I reach?
Reached this place with amazingly bright lights
Moving so fast I only see blurred visions of humans
Humans running around
Are they saving lives? I hope so
The shock of the fall hits me again
As I slip into a peaceful sleep, going numb everywhere.

The Alchemist

From extinguished lead to a glinting bag of gold
He could do it all
From the deathbed to the backyard
He could cure all.
Running through his mind like a river
Were thoughts about his...past?
Past that set fire to his memory
Something no magic could restore.
Now sitting in front of the holy cross
He had hazy memories of a girl with short locks of brown
Smiling up at him like he was god
God who could grant anything
And suddenly his vision flickers
And he's back in the room with no light
Flickering because of tears welling up in his eyes
Threatening to spill
Just like that man, that day
Threatening to spill his secret.

COLORS

Everything around me is of the same color
Confused, I walk along the path and with every step
A stone turns black
Black from yellow
And another turns red
And another turns gray
Confused yet again, I take a leaf and touch it
And the leaf shivers
Shivers like it has feelings
Feelings of a hurt human heart
And that's when I realized where I was
It was my mind
And everything I touched or came in contact with
Lost its beauty
Everything I loved shivered at my touch
As a tear slipped
I walked away into the darkness, and fell into a deep slumber.

HALO

She told me this is right where it began
As she clutches my arms and recites a poem
A poem that probably showed me
Who she really was
As her grip got tighter on my arm
The halo over hair head disappeared
And her eyes turned red
This scared me but I remained calm
And smiled with every sentence she said
As her nails dug deep into my skin
I knew my fate was as bad as the situation
She kept talking as if unaware
Of what she was doing to me
I pretended to fall, when she stood over me
I pulled her down and laughed
The real evil here being me
And not her with her disappearing halo and red eyes.
She was becoming human and I, the devil.

Skyscrapers

Trying to catch a glimpse of this giant
I am reminded of a version of myself
Trying to catch a glimpse of my father's face
Looking up the same way I look up at this skyscraper
As I ascend the staircase
I am reminded of running up the slide
Back home with the colorful wood
And beautiful designs
And as I climbed it I would feel the wood under my fingers
And smile to myself thinking, it will be beautiful forever
And as I climbed the stairs, my hand felt the familiar wood
I frowned because I really did know what wood it was
I looked down at my hand and a small design appeared from under my finger
I looked up and a man stood there
Dressed as crisp as possible with a forced smile on his face
Dad? I said.

All I Want

All I wanted was to hold you
Close to my heart where I could assure you
Assure you everything would be alright
But you ran
Ran away as far as possible
And I still remember feeling nervous
About having to run around the whole world
To get you back
But I didn't
Because the love in my heart told me,
Assured me that you'd come back
Or be happy, wherever you were.
Come back once, please?
That's all I want, I say to myself
No one close by to hear
I cry and cry
No one nearby to comfort me.

THE NINETY-FIFTH LETTER

He drank and drank, without any regret
For only he know the sadness he had faced
A small boy, his small boy, said
I think you drink too much, with a small frown on his face
And the father replied, I think you're right
But nothing could be done when he saw
All the trophies lined up on the shelf
Bragging their victories of the games he'd won
The games he'll never be able to play again.
He drank and drank, without any happiness
As if someone was forcing him to drink
But his family despised the new him
And it is sad, he whispered
Now in a room with just one window and one bed
Where someone would come every day to talk to him
Even when he didn't want to
And he sent his ninety fifth letter to his son, apologizing

Take my Body

She wept and wept
Begging for him to take her body
Elsewhere where no one would see
Somewhere no one would know
He didn't know what to do
He stood there
In the deafening silence
And thought about what his wife wanted him to do
My wife is crying, my wife is dying
He whispered to himself
Somewhere no one could hear him
Somewhere no one could find him
He watched her roll over and move to his side
And clutch his hand with confidence he failed to gather
And smiled and closed her eyes
And fell into a sleep he couldn't wake her out of
He woke up to find her gone, and a little blood around.

Fresh Dirt from an Old Grave

I visit you everyday
Since the day I pulled the plug
Since the day you let go of my hand
I visit you every week
Remembering your cookies
Remembering your voice
I visit you every month
Thinking about your sweet face
Thinking about your hugs
I visit you every year
My memory fading
But as the wind blew dirt in my face
I remembered only then
It was fresh dirt from an old grave.

GRACEFUL

As the dark clouds set in
I walk to that tree
The tree that once gave me shelter
From all the injustice
All the crimes
All the unfairness
I walk to there because I know
It'd give me shelter from the sky.
But as the drops of rain hit the stones
Music sounds
Music that reaches only my ears
Music that's got my limbs
Limbs moving gracefully
I outstretch my arm, and help a branch
I stretch my leg and push back a root in place
Making the tree complete
I am content.

WAVES

Gushing to the shore
Pushing each other out of the way as if it was a race
Trying to reach my pink toes
And for once in my life
I felt wanted
I moved back a step, and they still kept coming
This is fun, I thought
I touched the water with my finger
And I felt a tingle up my spine
A smile spread across my face
And I realized this was the happiest I felt in a long time
As I sat down to draw the beautiful sky
Someone came and laid their hands on my shoulder
I turned around and faced a small girl with a button nose
She smiled at me like I was her whole life
Hi mom! She said
I hugged her as she sang one of the songs she learnt.

PENNED

As the pen touches the paper
She knew exactly what
Her mind voiced
Voiced her heart
Hand mimicked her mind
As she wrote the words
She smiles because she knows
Her words maybe reality
Reality one day
But until then
The unanimity of her voice
The sound of her laughter
The smoothness of her face
The happiness in her eyes
Are all the world thinks she writes about.

The Chair

He takes his cup of tea with him to the very same chair
The chair that had been with him
Since he got his first white hair
He sat on it and smiled
As if the chair spoke to him
Spoke to him about some things
He can't speak of
Spoke to him of what his wife, my mom
Might be doing right at this moment
He strokes the chair softly
As if it were some delicate animal
And sips his tea with utmost care, not spilling a drop
On his chair.
And as I sat and observed all this
I smiled to myself thinking about
All the losses he faced
And yet he smiles like he's the happiest ever.

A certain sadness had taken over her face
and I thought maybe
I was the reason she shed tears during her own wedding
and maybe I couldn't do anything to fix the sadness
and all I ever did was make it worse
Everytime she saw me
She looked as if a new wound was being opened
deep inside her body
Filling the empty voids with blood,
The voids that I was supposed to fill
The voids that were once her happiness

Climbing and climbing
Climbing atop the mountain
The mountain of stone
The mountain that shone.
I can't do it, I cried
I won't do it, but I tried
I tried and tried and until
Until I looked around and stopped
The beauty was breathtaking
The air was life giving.
A voice behind me said
This is only the half of it.
And the soft voice had a firmness
A hidden firmness
That told me to not give up.
Climbing and climbing
I finally reached the top
And as I lay down
With my arms wide open
As a free bird would do
I felt nothing but happiness
And purity, and an absence of sorrow.

Everyday discovering something new,
I realise I'm different,
Different from what I said and did a year ago,
Different from how I looked a year ago,
Different from the people I loved a year ago.
What did happen to us? you may ask,
and I simply said, change.
Change makes me, without you.

There's no end, there's no goodbye.
All we have is the memories left to us;
In the hope of re-enacting them once again,
Like a mere Shakespearean play.
We leave their world, waiting to be remembered again,
Because that's how we find comfort,
Comfort in someone regretting letting you go.
But tell me this, isn't that evil of us?
Making them suffer, by leaving?

His eyes lit up
at the sight of me in the doorway
with two bags and a small smile
letting him know I was back for good
he hugged me and it felt
like he had longed for me
and I realised I felt the same way
when I hugged him back;
I pulled back as a tear fell on his cheek
Hi grandpa, I said.

She turned the key in the lock,
and hopes to walk into happiness,
Instead she receives betrayal and
a sound that shows how broken she is.
We waited too long, a voice said,
And the smile slipped off her face like red leaves in fall.
Let it all go, her mind said,
and yet another voice spelled out revenge.
Amidst a conflict like this she walks away,
and knew not where to go.

Leave me alone, she said
I don't move, standing there looking
Looking at her miserable state
Leave me alone, she repeated
Repeated more firmly.
But I stand there as though
As though I was a tree
Tree in a storm of tears
Tears tearing nothing down, but her.

~a~

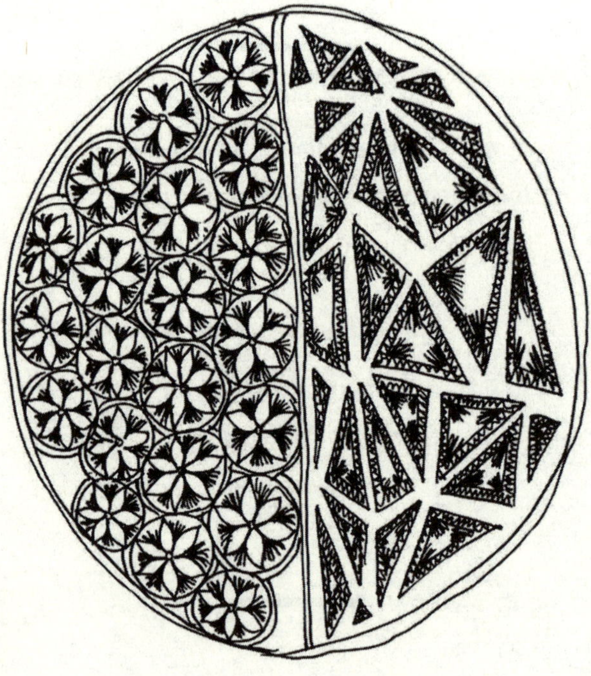

Exploring the paths I've lived
I see the amount of bloodshed caused
Just by a set of words let free
Let free from the cage holding hearts
Hearts with a cold cause.

~a~

Is there someone else watching
As you love me with all your will
Is there someone else listening
When you say I'm your world
Is there someone else crying
When you comfort me
Is there someone else smiling
When I cry because of you?

~a~

When she gracefully moves her body
With every note is a change in expression
With every word is a glint in her eye
With every step is a different kind of smile
When she dances
You don't know her insides
Is she sad? Is she angry?
You will never know
As with every song comes a newfound happiness
With every motion she spreads glee.

~a~

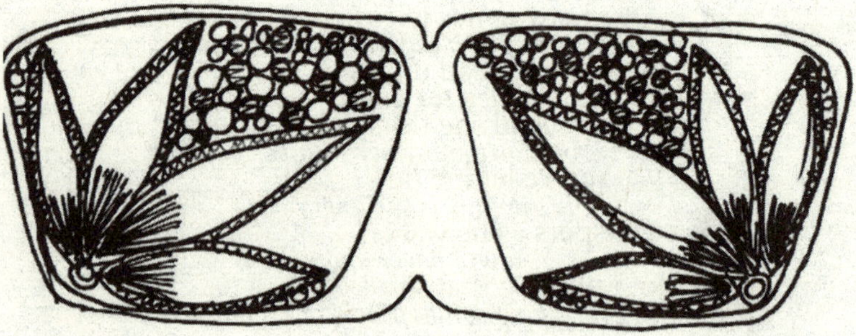

As she lays down
He moves
Letting her fall and hit
Hit her head on the stone
And she thought
You've let me down again
She whispers as he walks away smirking
Not knowing that she was the wave
That'd later cause the flood.

~a~

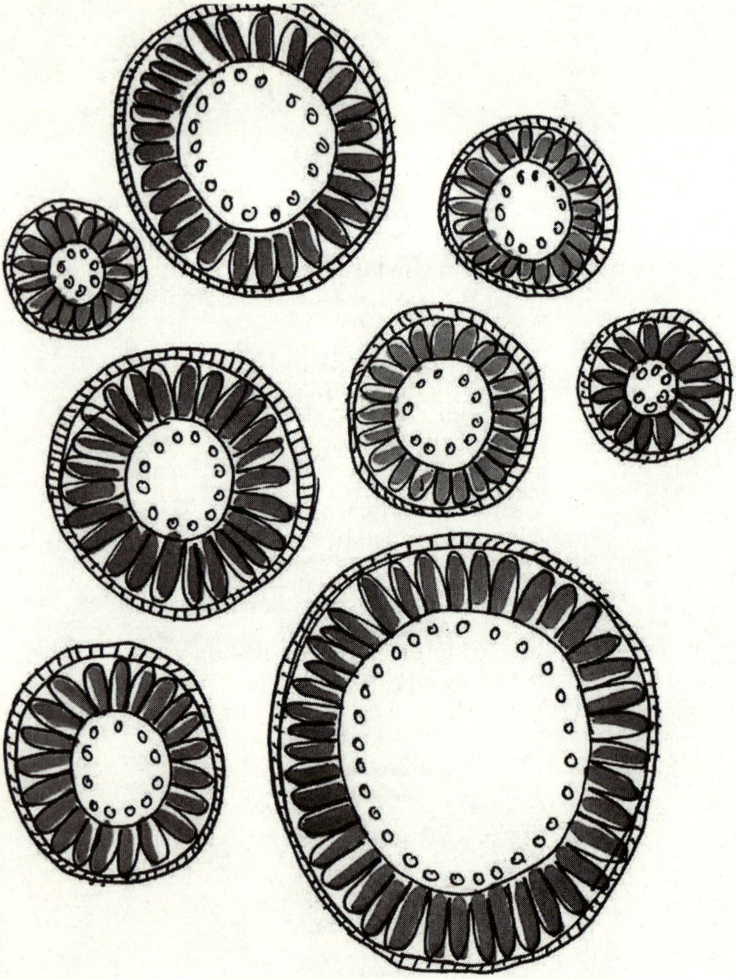

She said her good-bye, waving and smiling
Unaware of the tear travelling down her cheek
She knew she'd miss them
All of them, from the dog to the gray haired lady
And yet she left, because she knew
Loneliness was what drove her to who she was
And being surrounded by the people she loved
The people who loved her
Only reminded her of the sins she committed
Her loved ones, still unaware.

~a~

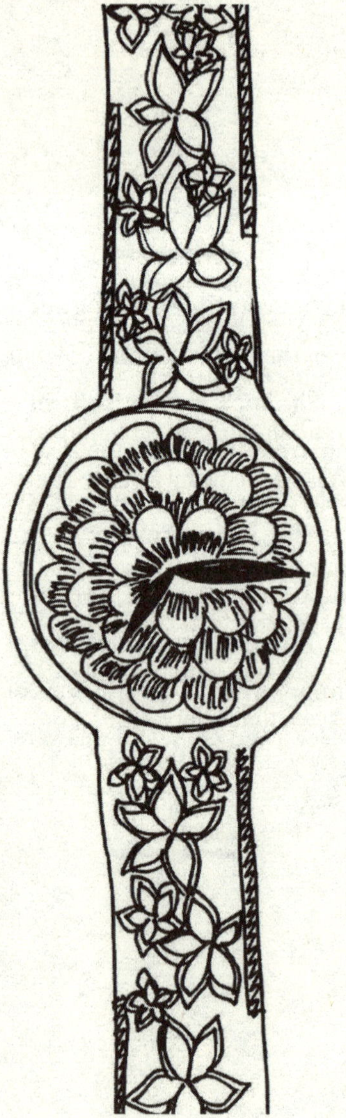

Let's run away to safety
Where earth transforms
Into the slightest slivers of heaven
Where the beauty of a smile
Cannot be compared to life
Where love is greater than evil
And we can run away
From everyone who made us believe
Believe that safety didn't exist.

~a~

Love will set you free, they said
And yet now it held her captive
Captive with confusion and guilt
Guilt of the absence of love
But a sense of freedom
From the strings controlling her
Strings of honesty
About her other lover.

~a~

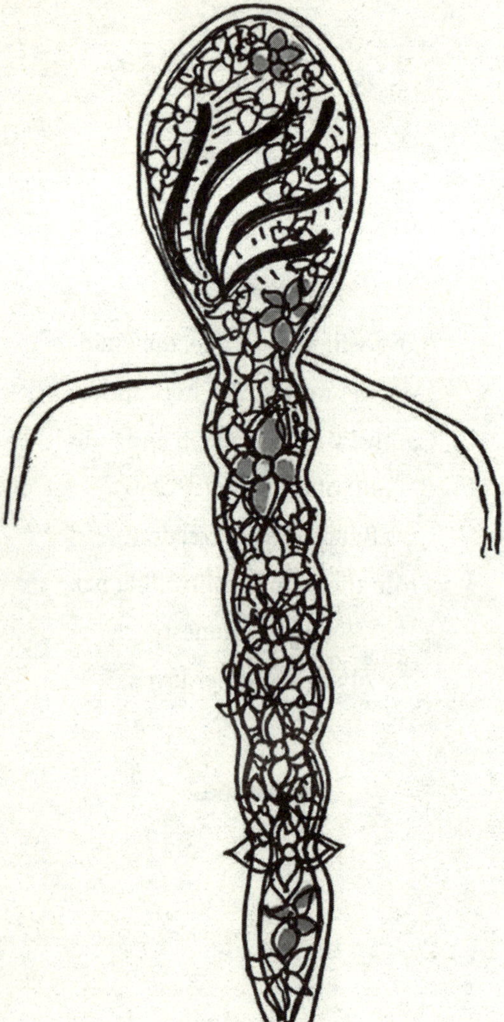

Broken bottles with smeared blood
Are picked up and cleaned with no emotion
But only she knows
How the glass went through her
As tears of pain spilt in sync with blood
As the bottle returned out
She let her hand hold her hand
As she left to a better place.

~a~

Acknowledgements

I would like to thank my parents for making this dream come true.

I would like to thank my mentors, Ranjini aunty and Neeraj uncle, for driving me to make this possible.

I would also like to thank Aditya Suryanarayanan for the first art piece in the book.

And last but never the least, I would like to thank Pblishing.com and all my friends who have helped me reach this far.

ABOUT THE AUTHOR

Aadithi Arasu

date of birth 22 November-2000

place of birth Princeton, New Jersey, USA.

I am a sixteen-year-old who loves to write. I started reading when I was almost eleven, and I had no intentions of writing back then. When I was fifteen I discovered a talent in me that I had no idea about, and till now I have put it to effective use. Publishing a book was never on my bucket list, but now all I can think about is my next book. I aspire to major in something related to international affairs and communications.

you can write to the author @
aadiyam20000@gmail.com

follow the author
https://www.facebook.com/profile.php?id=100011417259240

Crowd-Funders

(names listed alphabetically)

- Aaushi Agrawal
- Aditya D Menon
- Akash M N
- Akshaya Jebakumar
- Amlan Dad
- Ananya Ivaturi
- Aparna Bansal
- Archana Chitta
- Archana Reddy
- Aryan Kota
- Beenaa M Keshava
- Bhaktha Naidu
- Bhanuchandar Ketireddi
- Brijesh Bhatia
- Dishita Srivastava
- Experis IT
- Frane Bhattacharya
- Gopikrishna Kannan
- Govardhani Jasti
- Hanuma Yellinedi
- Harish Kumar
- Jyotsna R
- Kaarthic Sathyamurthy
- Koya Ravikanth
- Kusuma Raju
- Madhavi Koneru
- Medha Ajay
- Murali Balasubramaniam
- Nesha Prabahar
- Nisha Santhosh
- Nitya D
- Phani Ambarapu
- Pooja Chopra
- Prasad Devadiga
- Pratik Agarwal
- Priyai S
- Raghuraman Chandrasekaran
- Rajesh Murugan
- Rakesh Mohan
- Ramesh Jampula
- Ranjini Rao
- Ranjini Sridhar
- Rashmi Jha
- Ravi Ganti
- Sai Prapanch Adloori
- Samuel Christopher
- Santoshi G
- Satish Kotala
- Satyaraj Mayor
- Sethu Lambu
- Shaik Gouse
- Shailaja Rao Mushunuri
- Shoba Ashok
- Srinivas Raju R
- Sujatha Idiculla
- Sunidhi Bansal
- Sushmitha Shankar
- Syed Ahmed
- Tanvi Desai
- Tashi Lhamu
- Teja Manakame
- Thiru Shama
- Thiruchendhil Arasu (TC-Dell)
- Ukn Esperanza 1
- Vamsi Ayyagari
- Venkata Hari Krishna Linga
- Venkateswara Kolluri
- Vibhu Dureha
- Vijay Sankar
- Vikram Nehra
- Vikrant Payal
- Vineetha Vijayakumar
- Vinoth M

the first readers said...

- **Miss Shefali Tyagi – Principal of National Public School, HSR Layout.**

  The emotions and feelings generated by the poems are realistic and soul stirring and thought provoking. It leaves one wanting for more and transports you to a make believe world of mixed emotions, which only a person with decades of experience can feel. The intensity of each poem depicts Aadithi's emotional strength and maturity quite beyond her age.

- **Cherry Khanna**

  I found the poems very moving. The visuals created by the words were very vivid and thought provoking. I wanted to read only one poem a day and spend time letting the words sink in. Some of the elicit emotions that we don't want to bring forward, but need to. I loved the depth of emotion that were stirred in me. Personally I could identify and connect with the author. They show a depth of perception very unusual for a 16 year old.

- **Ranjini Rao – Independent Consultant and Senior mentor at Spark career Mentors.**

  This is a really unique way of Aadithi's way of expression through her poems and art. Each of her poems, depict emotion that convey a profound meaning. I wish her all the best in her journey into writing.

- **Miss Nisha – Teacher at NPS HSR**

  The poems are vivid, heart-warming and an absolute delight to read.

- **Neeraj Khanna**

  16 years old Aadithi has shown early signs of a top writer in the making. Each of her poems is unique and brilliantly crafted. This book represents the potential and power of 'India's Teen Turks'!